T0400709

WORLD'S FASTEST CARS

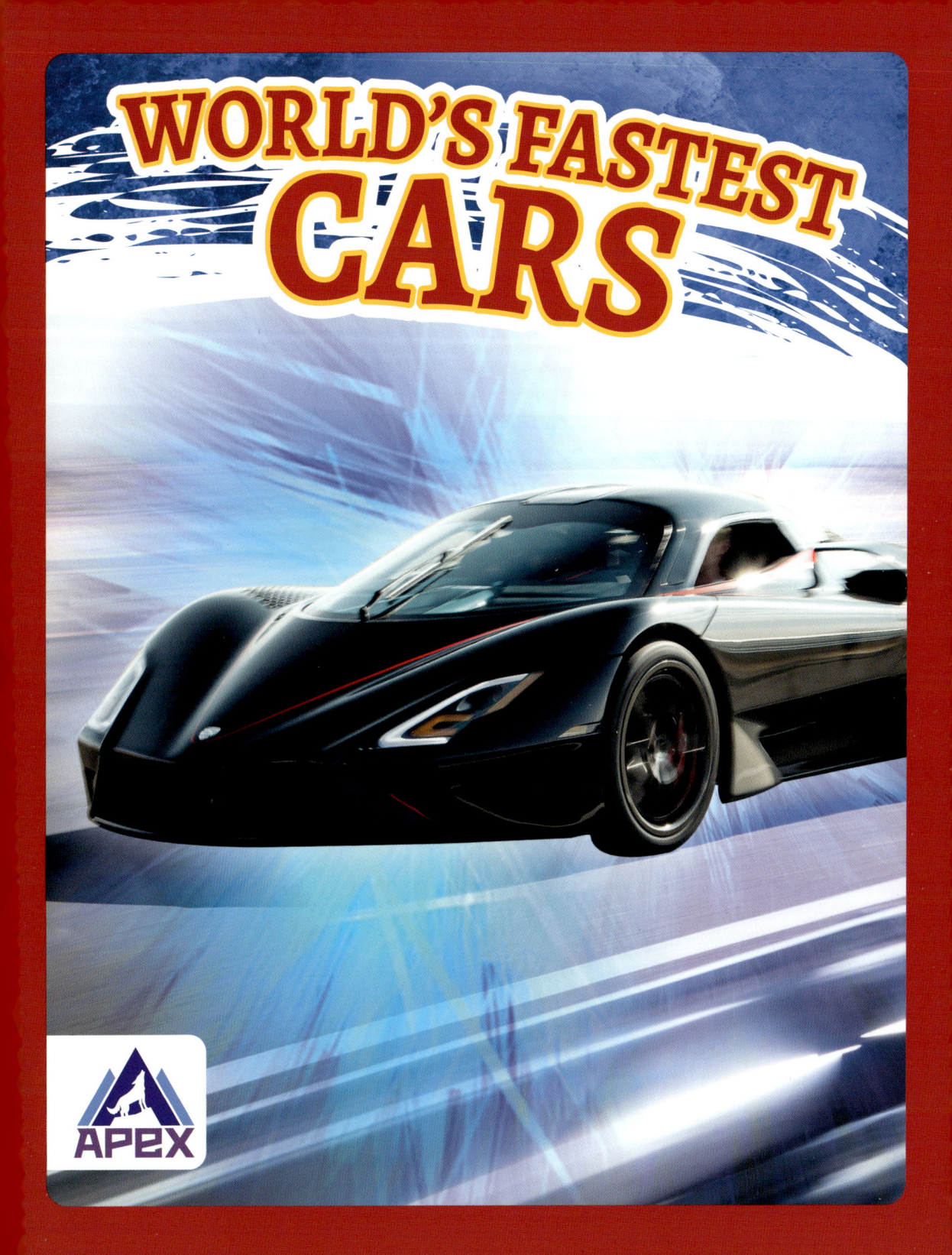

BY HUBERT WALKER

WWW.APEXEDITIONS.COM

Apex is distributed by North Star Editions:
sales@northstareditions.com | 888-417-0195

Produced for Apex by Red Line Editorial.

Photographs ©: Cover Images/AP Images, cover, 1; SSC/MEGA/Newscom, 4–5; James Lipman/Jameslipman.Com/Zuma Press/Newscom, 6–7, 8–9; Shutterstock Images, 10–11, 13, 14–15, 16–17, 18, 19, 20–21, 21, 22–23, 24–25, 26–27, 27, 29; Bain News Service/ Library of Congress, 12

Library of Congress Control Number: 2021918403

ISBN
978-1-63738-170-0 (hardcover)
978-1-63738-206-6 (paperback)
978-1-63738-274-5 (ebook pdf)
978-1-63738-242-4 (hosted ebook)

Printed in the United States of America
Mankato, MN
012022

NOTE TO PARENTS AND EDUCATORS

Apex books are designed to build literacy skills in striving readers. Exciting, high-interest content attracts and holds readers' attention. The text is carefully leveled to allow students to achieve success quickly. Additional features, such as bolded glossary words for difficult terms, help build comprehension.

TABLE OF CONTENTS

CHAPTER 1

BLAZING SPEED

A driver **revs** the engine of his SSC Tuatara. In just a few seconds, the car reaches 60 miles per hour (97 km/h).

The SSC Tuatara took nearly 10 years to design and build.

The Tuatara continues to pick up speed. The car's engine screams.

For safety, a driver tests the Tuatara's speed on a closed road. No other cars are on this road.

The Tuatara first went on sale in 2020. It cost $1.6 million.

Soon, the car goes nearly 280 miles per hour (451 km/h). The driver comes to a stop. Then he makes another run. This time, he reaches 286 miles per hour (460 km/h).

HYPERCARS

The world's fastest cars are known as hypercars.

They are very rare. They are also very expensive.

Hypercars are hard to control at high speeds.

Only skilled drivers can use them.

In 2021, the Tuatara set a record for fastest average speed over two runs.

CHAPTER 2

FAST CARS THROUGH HISTORY

The Benz Velo was one of the first cars ever made. It came out in the 1890s. Its top speed was only 12 miles per hour (20 km/h).

In its first eight years, the Benz Velo was a top-selling car. About 1,200 Benz Velo cars were sold.

Cars improved quickly. In 1905, a car reached 100 miles per hour (161 km/h). By the 1950s, the fastest cars could go 150 miles per hour (241 km/h).

The "Blitzen Benz" was the world's fastest car for most of the 1910s. It reached a top speed of more than 140 miles per hour (225 km/h).

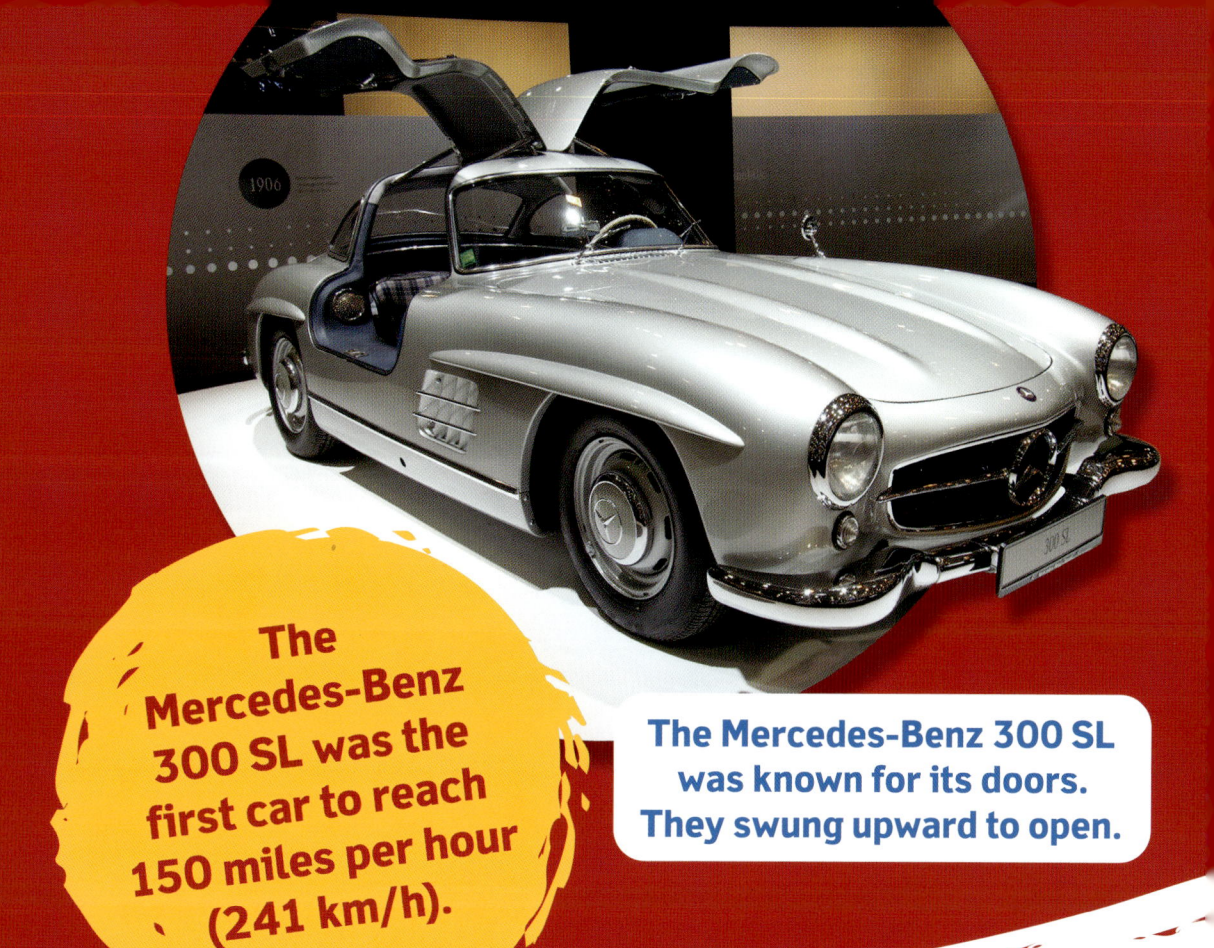

The Mercedes-Benz 300 SL was the first car to reach 150 miles per hour (241 km/h).

The Mercedes-Benz 300 SL was known for its doors. They swung upward to open.

NOT SO FAST

In 1896, a driver got the world's first speeding ticket. He was going 8 miles per hour (13 km/h). A police officer chased him down on a bicycle.

By the late 1980s, the fastest cars could top 200 miles per hour (322 km/h). One was the Ferrari F40. Another was the Porsche 959S.

A Porsche 959 (left) gets ready to race a Ferrari F40.

CHAPTER 3

DESIGN IMPROVEMENTS

Light cars can go faster than heavy cars. So, car **designers** use the lightest materials possible.

The McLaren F1 is hundreds of pounds lighter than the Ferrari F40.

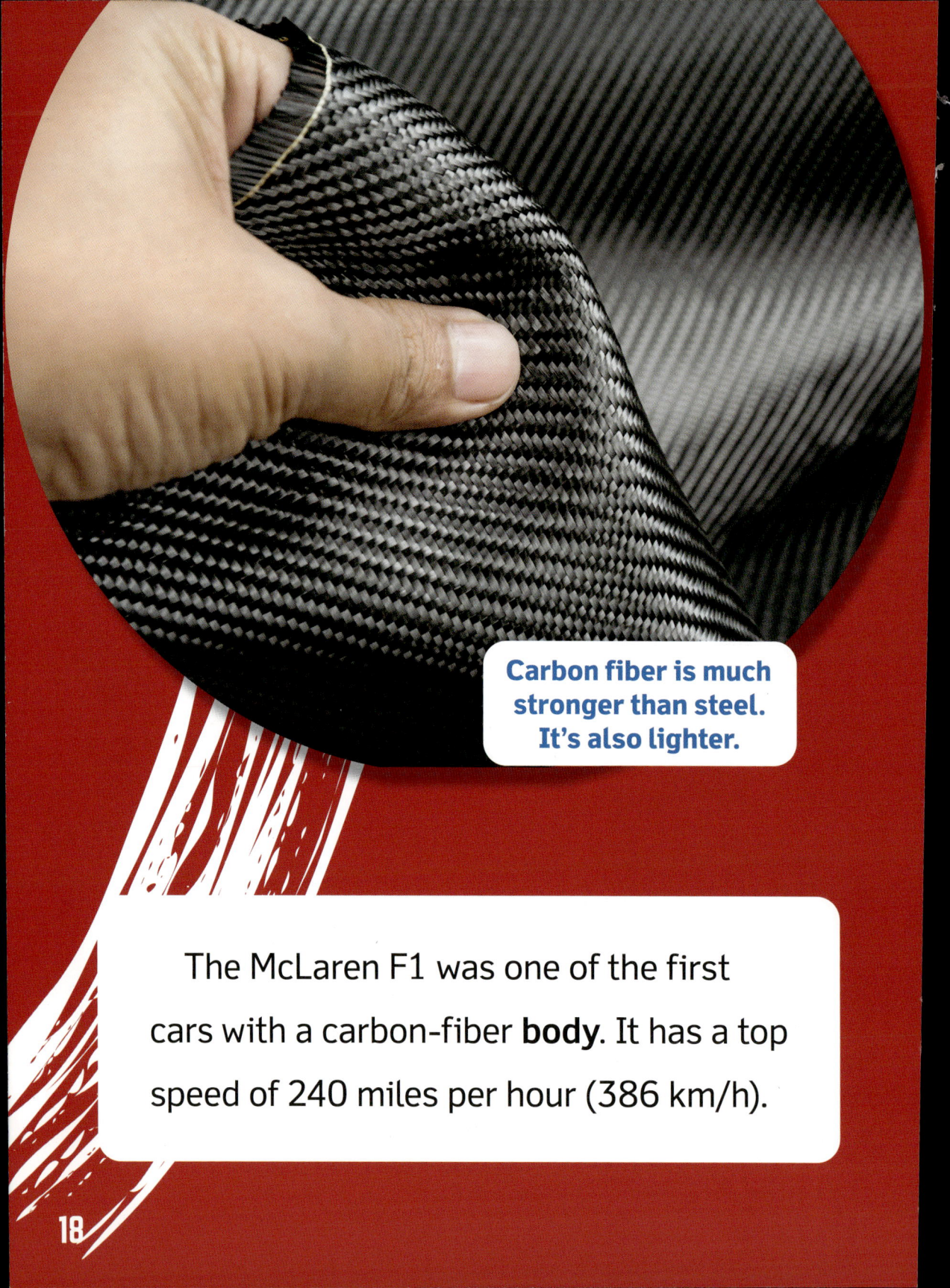

Carbon fiber is much stronger than steel. It's also lighter.

The McLaren F1 was one of the first cars with a carbon-fiber **body**. It has a top speed of 240 miles per hour (386 km/h).

The McLaren F1 can go from 0 to 60 miles per hour (0–97 km/h) in 3.2 seconds.

Bumpers made from carbon fiber can help cars move faster.

The Koenigsegg Agera RS uses two **turbochargers**. These parts help the engine produce more power.

The Koenigsegg Agera RS can hit 278 miles per hour (447 km/h).

Modern hypercars use paddle shifters on the steering wheel to change gears.

Many sports cars have spoilers on the back.

SPOILERS

A car spoiler pushes air upward. As a result, the car is pushed downward. A spoiler helps keep the car on the road when it's going fast.

CHAPTER 4

FASTER AND FASTER

Designers pay close attention to a car's shape. For example, the SSC Tuatara is shaped like a **wedge**. Air moves around the car easily.

Designers based the SSC Tuatara's shape off a fighter jet's.

23

Designers also use air to cool the car. The Bugatti Chiron has openings that send air to the engine. That way, the engine does not **overheat**.

The Bugatti Chiron Super Sport 300+ can top 300 miles per hour (483 km/h).

The Chiron's engine can produce 1,500 horsepower.

BUGATTI

Not all hypercars have gasoline engines. Some are powered by electricity. These cars can still reach speeds well over 200 miles per hour (322 km/h).

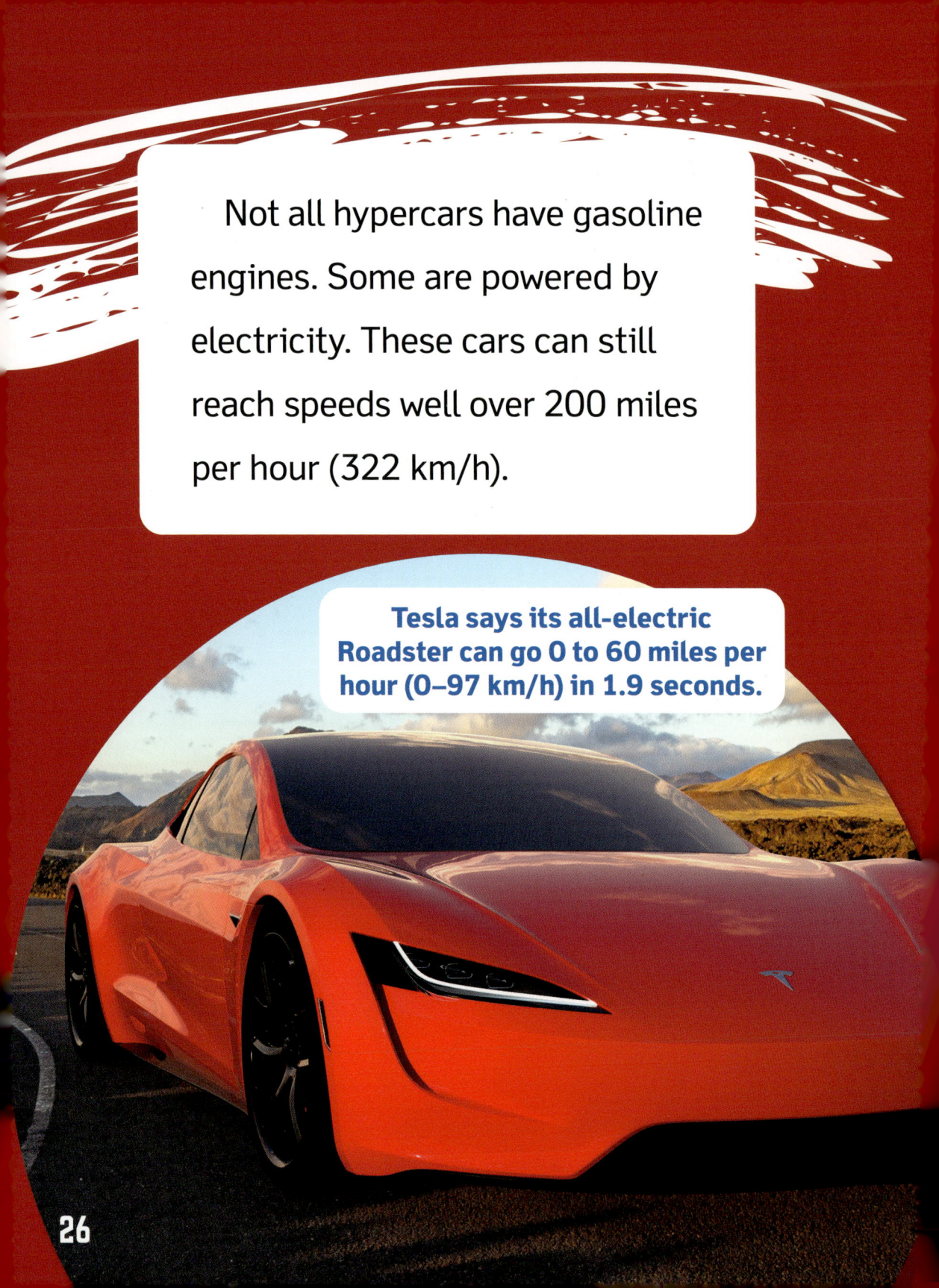

Tesla says its all-electric Roadster can go 0 to 60 miles per hour (0–97 km/h) in 1.9 seconds.

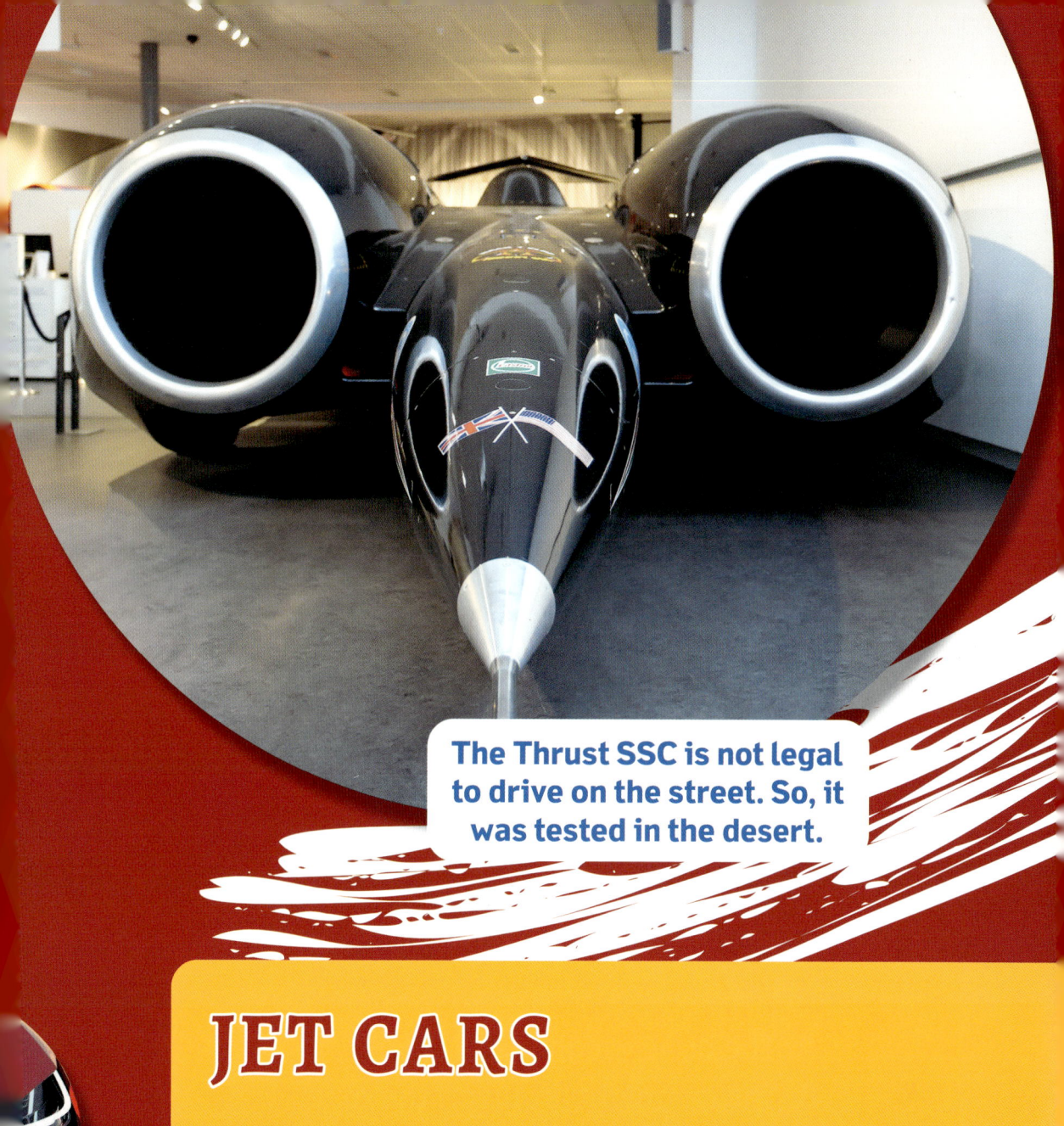

The Thrust SSC is not legal to drive on the street. So, it was tested in the desert.

JET CARS

Jet engines power the Thrust SSC. A driver tested this car in 1997. He went a record-setting 763 miles per hour (1,228 km/h).

COMPREHENSION QUESTIONS

Write your answers on a separate piece of paper.

1. Write a sentence that explains the main ideas of Chapter 2.

2. If you could ride in any hypercar, which one would you choose? Why?

3. When did cars reach speeds of 200 miles per hour (322 km/h) for the first time?

  A. 1890s
  B. 1950s
  C. 1980s

4. What might happen if a hypercar didn't have a spoiler?

  A. The driver might get a ticket.
  B. The car might lift up off the road.
  C. The engine might stop working.

5. What does **skilled** mean in this book?

*Hypercars are hard to control at high speeds. Only **skilled** drivers can use them.*

   A. good

   B. new

   C. slow

6. What does **materials** mean in this book?

*So, car designers use the lightest **materials** possible. The McLaren F1 was one of the first cars with a carbon-fiber body.*

   A. how much things weigh

   B. things that items are made from

   C. people who come up with ideas

Answer key on page 32.

GLOSSARY

body
The outer part of a car that gives the car its shape.

designers
People who come up with new ideas for products.

gears
Settings on a vehicle that control how fast it can go. Gears control how power moves from the vehicle's engine to its wheels.

horsepower
A unit that measures the power of engines and motors. A standard car engine usually has about 200 horsepower.

jet engines
Engines that create power by burning fuel mixed with air.

overheat
To stop working after getting too hot.

revs
Makes an engine speed up and work harder.

turbochargers
Parts that push more air into engines, helping the engines produce more power.

wedge
A shape that is thin on one end and thicker at the other end.

TO LEARN MORE

BOOKS

Doeden, Matt. *Sports Cars*. North Mankato, MN: Capstone Press, 2019.

Fishman, Jon M. *Cool Sports Cars*. Minneapolis: Lerner Publications, 2019.

Hamilton, S. L. *The World's Fastest Cars*. Minneapolis: Abdo Publishing, 2021.

ONLINE RESOURCES

Visit **www.apexeditions.com** to find links and resources related to this title.

ABOUT THE AUTHOR

Hubert Walker enjoys running, hunting, and going to the dog park with his best pal. He grew up in Georgia but moved to Minnesota in 2018. Overall, he loves his new home, but he's not a fan of the cold winters.

INDEX

Answer Key:
1. Answers will vary; **2.** Answers will vary; **3.** C; **4.** B; **5.** A; **6.** B